Cheeko's Island Adventure

J.D. Hoult

Illustrated by Stuart Thomson

Published in 2015 by FeedARead.com Publishing

Copyright ©J.D. Hoult 2004
Cheeko's Adventure logo ©J.D. Hoult 2010, 2014

Front cover and illustrations by ©Stuart Thomson 2015

First Edition

cheekosadventure.com

Cheeko's Island Adventure

J.D. Hoult

Illustrated by Stuart Thomson

Contents

Welcome to Paradise!

The aeroplane's brakes screeched loudly as it hurtled down the runway. Not a sound could be heard from the passengers as they clung tightly onto their seats, until the plane came to an abrupt standstill, then everyone cheered with excitement and delight.

"Welcome to paradise!" announced the captain to another plane load of holidaymakers; having just landed on a beautiful island in the middle of the crystal clear ocean. This particular island was nicknamed Nectar Island for it surely was pure paradise.

As the sun shone down from high in the sky not a cloud could be seen and the sea sparkled like scattered crystals. Waves lapped gently against the perfect sandy beach that stretched all the way around the island, as far as the eye could see.

The sand was very fine and slipped gently through your toes as you walked on it. At times it would get so hot you had to run across the sand like a desert lizard so it wouldn't burn your feet. Strangely, there were hardly any shells to be found in the sand, only very tiny ones.

Huge palm and coconut trees were dotted all along the beach, towering above you and gently swaying in the warm tropical breeze. Occasionally the odd coconut would fall to the ground and if it wasn't swept out to sea by the waves, local people would make it into a souvenir carving of an animal or bird.

The holidaymakers stepped off the plane, collected their luggage and trundled off to make their way to their hotels, they were all very excited. If only they knew that this island used to be even more beautiful. They had no idea what sacrifices had been made just so they could visit this paradise island. It used to be totally deserted, unspoilt and peaceful, not a hotel in sight.

There used to be fields filled with sugar cane and if you climbed up on the hills and looked down, it resembled a green swaying ocean. It was a spectacular sight but all this had been destroyed.

The island's rainforest was now only half its size and hardly any animals lived there. It used to be the very heart of the island buzzing with insects and wildlife.

A lovely mangrove pond sat quaintly amongst the coconut and palm trees where all the animals once gathered on hot sunny days. The trees were always full of monkeys calling one another in their high-pitched chatter, whilst swinging from tree to tree.

It used to be such a lively place with lots of birds twittering and singing. Dragonflies buzzed, humming birds hummed and mongooses burrowed amongst leaves looking for berries and insects to eat. If you were an animal that was the place to be, living peacefully in the rainforest.

A family of little green monkeys had lived in the forest for many years. They were quite small with long curly tails and when the sun shone down on them their fur looked green. They had pale little faces and deep orange eyes and they would make a chattering sound to one another, which sometimes sounded as if they were laughing. This chatter could be heard for miles around, echoing throughout the forest.

Their home had been near the mangrove pond in a secluded part of the forest. Each monkey had their own little tree house, built with their own bare hands from the delights of the rainforest. They were very proud and protective of their home and were a very close family.

The little family of monkeys had been very happy, life being simple and full of fun with no enemies. Their only quarrel would have been with the mongoose family, pinching their juicy berries when the monkeys weren't looking.

At the head of the family was the father, his name was Miguel and he was very well respected. When he said jump, the others jumped. Miguel was quite a big monkey and fairly old, in fact his fur was now more grey than green. He only had one front tooth left, so had to eat ripe, mashed up fruit.

The mother was called Tulum. She too was quite old but was still a beautiful monkey, with an air of grace about her like a Queen.

Anya was the daughter, she was the eldest and was quite bossy and very lazy. Anya struggled to swing from the trees, always missing branches and ending in a heap on the floor. This amused her three brothers; Coco, Maddy and Cheeko, tremendously.

Coco and Maddy were nicknamed the terrible twins. They were always in trouble together and never went anywhere without each other.

The youngest monkey was Cheeko, who was also the smallest in the family and slightly different from the others. His fur was a lot greener and you didn't need the sun shining down on him to see how green he was. He also had black spiky hair on the top of his head and a white tip on the end of his long curly tail.

Cheeko's most striking features were his big brown sad looking eyes, not orange like the others, but beautiful brown eyes with long dark eyelashes. His chatter was also very high-pitched and stood out from all the rest.

Cheeko was definitely a very special little monkey and was quite a character, always the playful, mischievous one. His mother would call him Cheeky Cheeko as he flashed his big brown eyes at her when he had been mischievous. She always had trouble scalding him when he fluttered his long eyelashes, looking so cute.

Cheeko liked nothing more than to play games with his brothers and sister. They would swing amongst the tall trees chasing one another, laughing and screeching. They would also have races together, running up a coconut tree and the first one to grab a coconut won, the losers would have to do a forfeit. Luckily for Cheeko though he was always the fastest.

At night-time, when they had finished playing, the family would get together and dance and sing around an open fire, roasting berries and mango fruit on the end of a stick. Life was just so wonderful for this family of monkeys, they were all so happy.

Unfortunately, as the saying goes, all good things must come to an end and that's just what happened. One fateful day life for the animals on this peaceful tropical island changed forever, never to be the same again. This is the story of that day and Cheeko's island adventure.

Chapter 2

Paradise Lost

It was summer-time and Cheeko awoke with a loud yawn and a long stretch. The sun beamed down from above on his shiny green fur. It was his turn to collect breakfast from the rainforest so he was up and about before the others.

After walking a short distance into the forest he came upon large juicy berries and fresh sweet mango fruit, which he began to collect and put in a large basket made from banana leaves. Now all he needed was the succulent sweet milk from large coconuts that his family loved to drink.

Using his natural monkey skills Cheeko climbed right to the top of a large coconut tree, wrapped his feet around a branch and turned upside down. As he dangled high above the ground he grabbed a coconut with both hands and dropped it to the floor. Using his long curly tail he then grabbed another branch, turned upright and made his way down the tree trunk safely to the bottom.

By now Cheeko had gathered enough food for breakfast and had placed everything in his large banana leaf basket. He picked it up with both arms, held it out in front of him and started to make his way home. It was very large and top heavy for a little monkey like Cheeko and he could not see over it.

As Cheeko tried to carry the basket he looked like a pile of wobbly fruit, with two little legs sticking out from the bottom. He banged into trees and bushes and ended up in a heap on the floor, buried under fruit and coconuts, with his little head poking out of the top.

It used to take him twice as long as the others to collect breakfast. Eventually he arrived home in time for his mother to prepare a healthy breakfast feast for all the family, it was always delicious.

After breakfast Cheeko decided he was going to make his way down to the mangrove pond to collect dragonflies. He wanted to play one of his favourite games with his brothers called 'race the dragon.'

Each brother held a dragonfly and on the count of three they would let them go and the first one to fly across a long reed, tied between two trees, was the winner. Cheeko first had to catch them which could take a while as they were very smart dragonflies and were also quite big and buzzed very loudly.

The mangrove pond was only a short distance away and once there Cheeko had to be very quiet. He tiptoed daintily across the large lilies in the middle of the pond, trying not to fall in. This is where the dragonflies would rest in the sunshine.

Cheeko stood on a large lily, took a massive deep breath and leapt across the pond, pouncing on a dragonfly. There was a huge splash as he belly flopped into the water. He had completely missed the dragonfly which turned around, stared at him, buzzed very loudly and then flew off in disgust.

Cheeko was not going to give up and after several attempts managed to catch enough dragonflies to be able to play his game. Although he still had to get across the pond whilst holding onto the dragonflies, balancing on the lily leaves and trying not to fall in at the same time. This was going to be very difficult as they wriggled and tickled his hands.

Cheeko carefully placed his tiny feet on the lily leaves and strode slowly across. Occasionally he ended up balancing on one leg as he wobbled, clasping his cupped hands tightly so as not to lose the dragonflies.

By the time he reached the edge of the pond he was soaking wet from belly flopping into the water and looked like a little wet rat. He put the dragonflies safely inside two coconut shells and held them together by tying a reed around them.

Cheeko decided to get himself dry before setting off for home and lay under a tall swaying palm tree in the warm tropical sun. All he could hear was the gentle sound of the waves in the distance and the monkeys in the trees calling to one another. It was so peaceful he nodded off to sleep.

After a few hours dozing Cheeko started to twitch and whimper in his sleep, as if he was having a nightmare. In this nightmare he could hear loud banging and clanking noises with voices shouting to one another in a language he hadn't heard before.

Cheeko started to shiver as a big black cloud hovered above his head, making it very dark and cold. He awoke startled at his horrible dream, expecting it to go away, but all the noises carried on and the big black cloud was still there.

Cheeko looked up in the sky and to his horror staring down at him was a big yellow monster that had a long arm and a giant claw at the end. The monster was moving closer and closer to Cheeko, as it did the trees surrounding him shook.

Terrified monkeys suddenly began running out from the shaking trees with their eyes wide open, fur standing up on end, waving their arms in the air; they were all fleeing for their lives. Beautiful butterflies, mosquitoes and moths formed a giant cloud that filled the sky as they all fled from the trees.

Baby monkeys clung to their mother's chest as they darted away from danger. In the entire commotion a baby monkey let go of his grip from around his mother and was left screeching in the middle of the stampede. Luckily his mother heard his cries and ran back to collect him, just in the nick of time as the monster's gigantic feet were upon them. It was sheer chaos with animals running in all directions screeching and whaling.

The monster began pushing over the tree Cheeko had been snoozing under. It came crashing down with a loud creak and giant thud as it hit the forest floor. Then without warning the monster's long arm came hurtling towards the ground, its giant claw scooping everything up in its path.

Cheeko turned and ran as fast as he could, not looking behind him. He ran and ran until he reached home, where he immediately told his family what he had seen. At first they thought it was Cheeko playing a trick and didn't believe him. But they soon started to believe him when they saw that he was shaking like a leaf with fear and his big brown eyes were wide open with terror.

Being head of the family Miguel immediately took charge. "We must call a forest meeting with all the animals and warn them, making sure we all stick together, for I fear our beloved island home is being invaded by something terrible."

That night a forest meeting was held and all the animals attended. Monkeys, birds, mongooses, bats, worms and tree frogs, they were all there and each took it in turns to keep watch during the long dark night. No one slept at all and you could feel the fear in the air, but all the animals stuck together putting any differences they had aside.

The night seemed to go on forever until finally the sun poked her head up on the horizon and it was daylight at last. The animals breathed a sigh of relief for they felt safer in daylight, but who knows what lay ahead for them and their beloved forest home?

"We must all eat something and keep up our strength," insisted Tulum. "For if our forest is to be taken away from us, we do not know when or where we shall find food. We must gather what we can in our banana baskets, making sure we stick together at all times."

Everyone agreed and each one of them took a banana leaf basket and ventured into the forest together to gather food supplies. Cheeko and his family worked hard to collect food quickly, as they were all very scared. After a short time their baskets were full to the brim with mangos, juicy red berries and coconuts.

The family started to make their way back home. Cheeko as usual was last, bumping into everything and looking more like a walking fruit bowl than a little green monkey. He was quite a distance behind the others, who were all nearly home. It was then Cheeko started to think about what he had seen yesterday at the mangrove pond.

Feeling brave and curious he decided he wanted to go and take a peep at what was happening. He knew it would be very dangerous, but curiosity had got the better of him. Cheeko needed to understand what was going on for the sake of the rainforest and his family. He put his basket down behind a large berry bush and tiptoed off in the direction of the mangrove pond.

As Cheeko got closer to the pond he could smell something funny in the air. It was a smell he had never experienced before, like burning twigs. He could also hear the same loud noises he had heard yesterday, clunking, banging and voices in a funny language. It was all very strange and bewildering for him.

Cheeko hid behind a bush and peeped around it to see what was going on. He saw tall two-legged, funny looking creatures with yellow things on their heads that looked like half coconuts. They were walking about and shouting at one another.

There was a big raging fire right in front of Cheeko and his beloved trees were being thrown upon it, gone forever. The heat started to singe the fur on Cheeko's ears and his monkey senses told him it wasn't safe to hang around.

Not liking what he saw he began to move away and head quickly for home. Just as he did so the big yellow monster with the long arm appeared. It stopped, turned around with its giant feet and brought down its scary claw, grabbing the bush Cheeko was hiding behind, almost scooping him up with it. Cheeko ran for his life, as fast as he could to collect his banana basket and head for home. That was a lucky escape he thought, it was very silly of him to have wandered away from the others like that, he would never do it again.

Cheeko ran back through the forest, until he reached the bush where he had hidden his basket. He rested for a second against a tree to try and catch his breath. He had never run so fast in all his life, not even whilst playing games with his brothers. After he had got his energy back he picked up his basket and wobbled off towards home.

For a while he kept on bumping into things as usual, as he couldn't see over his basket. As Cheeko got closer to home he stopped bumping into trees. This seemed very odd, as the trees where he lived were big and magnificent with large trunks and very close together. Strange thought Cheeko, I must be getting very good at carrying my basket, I'm not bumping into anything.

Even more bewildering to Cheeko was that the ground felt crunchy when he trod on it and every time he placed his foot down a crack echoed around the forest like a firecracker. There was also a funny smell in the air, a mixture of coconuts and wood.

Cheeko arrived home and put his basket down, looking up as he did so to call out to his mother, but instead he gave out a loud shriek with horror. Cheeko rubbed his little eyes in disbelief, the trees around him were totally destroyed and all piled up to one side. Coconuts were smashed into little pieces and scattered amongst the forest, their sweet fresh milk oozing out, filling the air with a strong coconut smell.

The trees that he used to swing from with his brothers lay broken all around him. Branches cracked and crunched under his tiny feet as he made his way through the devastation. The area was completely flat with no sign of his family or any other animal anywhere in sight, his family home was no more. The whole forest was being invaded by something terrible and it was closing in on Cheeko fast.

A ghostly silence filled the forest until Cheeko began frantically calling out to his family in his high-pitched chatter. He began running around desperately trying to find them. There was not even a dragonfly in sight; it was like a ghost town. Where would he go and where were his family?

Cheeko stood terrified in the middle of his flattened home, looking bewildered and scared. His eyes began to fill up and a large tear ran down his sweet cheek. He had never been on his own before and did not know what to do.

Cheeko wiped away his tear; he knew he had to be brave and strong to survive. At least he had his basket of food, so he would not starve. He pulled himself together and decided to head deeper into the forest where he hoped he would be safe.

Chapter 3

Cheeko Finds His Soul Mate

Cheeko ventured deeper into the forest, leaving behind the mangrove pond and his flattened home. Virtually no light shone through this part of the forest and all the trees had twisted scary looking branches. It was permanently dark, not pitch black, but as if the sun was just peeping through the thick branches. There was not a juicy berry or dragonfly in sight.

Cheeko and the animals never used to venture this deep into the forest, for everyone was scared. Cheeko's mother used to say to them; "never go beyond the bent over coconut tree for here is the start of the deep dark, scary forest. Strange goings on have happened beyond this point." Cheeko could see the strange looking bent over coconut tree just ahead of him and his knees began to knock with fright.

Cheeko took a deep breath, quickly put his fears aside and carried on dragging his basket of fruit behind him. He needed to be able to see where he was going and keep his wits about him. It was very heavy and his little arms by now were getting very tired, but he needed all the food he could get.

The forest did not look very inviting for a lonely little green monkey and he did not know what was waiting for him beyond the bent over coconut tree. Luckily he was only planning on staying a short while.

Cheeko dragged his basket as far as he could into the forest, he was by now exhausted and had plonked himself down on the floor. He looked up and a small ray of light beaming down caught his eye, it appeared to be shining on a friendly looking tree. It was the only tree that didn't have nasty twisted looking branches.

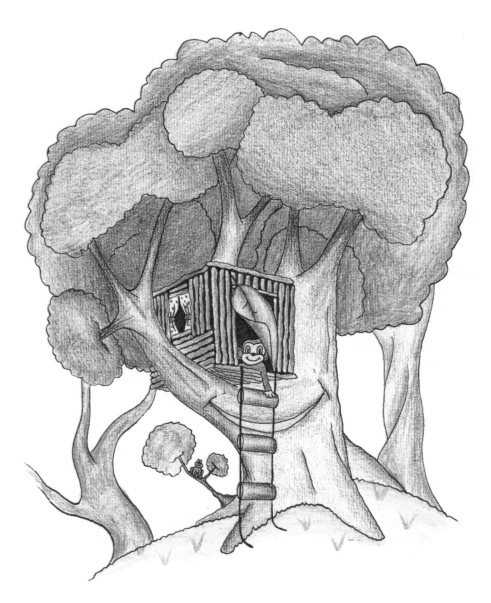

The tree looked like it was smiling at him, as it had a big cut in its trunk that looked like a large grin. He thought he would be safe here for a while and decided to build a little tree house high up the friendly tree. Cheeko began to unload his basket so he could use its banana leaves and reeds to help make his shelter.

Cheeko climbed high up into the tree and put together his shelter. He then started to collect his food from the ground, making several trips up and down until all his food was safely in his tree house. Using a large leaf he pulled it across his doorway and was safely tucked up inside.

It was Cheeko's first night in his tree house and he didn't sleep at all. There were a lot of strange noises in the forest that he hadn't heard before. He could hear things croaking loudly to one another and as the wind whistled through the trees it made a ghostly sound, almost like moaning.

At one point he poked his head out from behind his shelter, the sky was pitch black and he could see what looked like hundreds of eyes in the darkness. Cheeko quickly went back inside and made sure his door was secure.

It was a big relief when morning eventually came and again the ray of light shone down on his friendly tree. It was very strange that daylight never properly appeared in this part of the forest, only beaming down on Cheeko and his tree house.

Days eventually turned into weeks and Cheeko got used to the strange noises at night-time. There was not an animal in sight, not one monkey in the forest, just the ghostly whistling sounds through the trees.

Cheeko was getting used to being alone and would spend most of his days creating little animal sculptures made out of twigs from broken branches. He was starting to run out of food and knew he could not stay there much longer. Cheeko decided to spend one more night in the forest and then venture out to look for his family, as he missed them very much.

Cheeko's final night in the forest was about to become his worst. As night-time began to draw in he poked his head outside his tree house, took in a deep breath and sniffed the warm tropical air. There was a slight freshness about the night which meant only one thing, rain and lots of it.

Sure enough Cheeko's hunch was right, an almighty storm was brewing and in the early hours of the morning the rain began to lash down on Cheeko's tree house. The wind bellowed through his shelter and he had to use all his strength to try and hold it together. At one point, as he held on for dear life, both his legs were off the ground as if he was flying sideways.

Using an almighty surge of strength Cheeko managed to scramble back into his shelter and grab the door. He sat up against it to try and stop the wind coming in, but the raindrops were like big diamonds falling out of the sky and the wind got stronger and stronger.

Cheeko could hold his shelter together no more and with a large gust of wind it blew up in the air and disappeared into the sky. He grabbed hold of a large leaf as the wind whisked his home away and wrapped it around himself, the wind and rain lashing down on him as he hid underneath.

Eventually the storm died down and Cheeko unwrapped himself from beneath his leaf. He stood up, stretched his legs and shook himself to get dry, he was soaking wet.

Cheeko had managed to save one of his bananas so he ate that for his breakfast and started to make his way out of the forest. He was no longer afraid, having just spent thirty days and thirty nights in his tree house.

A small speck of fluorescent light perched on a log suddenly caught Cheeko's eye, it then disappeared into a puff of sparkling crystals. Thinking no more about it Cheeko continued on his way and trotted past the bent over coconut tree, deciding to head towards the mangrove pond, to begin searching for his family. They couldn't be too far away he thought.

As Cheeko got closer to the pond he started to creep very slowly, for he didn't know what he was going to find. Last time he was there the giant claw nearly scooped him up, he didn't want that to happen again.

Following his monkey instincts it led him to the exact place where his family home used to be. There was one coconut tree left standing so he hid behind it, slowly poking his head out to see what he could see.

Hearing loud noises he spotted lots of two-legged weird looking creatures with fuzzy hairdos. Some were jigging about to a loud thud thud, thud noise, they looked totally out of control.

Cheeko then noticed something large that looked like an enormous tree house. It was not made out of leaves and reeds, but brown blocks and it was so much bigger than the one Cheeko had made in the forest. He couldn't believe his eyes for it had appeared where he used to swing from the trees with his brothers, this was why his home had been destroyed and all the other animals' habitat sacrificed.

Devastated and confused, he stood watching silently for a few minutes and realised there was nothing he could do, his family home had been totally destroyed, gone forever.

Shaking his head in sadness he began to think about what he should do next when he was suddenly distracted by nice smells that made his tummy rumble, as by now he was becoming very hungry. Cheeko sniffed the air and began to follow his senses, creeping quietly on all fours along the floor, trying not to be noticed.

Eventually he came to a doorway where immediately in front of him were more two-legged creatures sitting down and other creatures bringing them food. Cheeko managed to sneak underneath where they were sitting. He thought no one could see him for he was under a table with a long white cloth hiding him.

A bit of food fell onto the floor near Cheeko's tail, he quickly gobbled it up, he was very hungry. It was a large piece of mango fruit and was very delicious, the best he'd ever tasted. It was so succulent the juice ran down his chin and made his fur all sticky, it reminded him of home.

Cheeko started to feel very sad and began daydreaming about happier times with his family. A sudden loud shriek brought him back to reality and made him jump with fright, causing him to bang his head on the table and whimper out loud. His tail had been poking out from underneath the table and he'd been spotted.

Before he knew it Cheeko was being chased away by the two-legged creatures. He ran swiftly over tables causing plates and cutlery to crash to the floor. There was lots of shrieking and commotion, it was sheer chaos, someone even tried to grab poor Cheeko's tail. Luckily he was too fast for them and managed to swing up to the roof and escape through a window that led down onto the beach. He carried on running as fast as he could until he could see he wasn't being chased anymore.

After his ordeal Cheeko sat down on the fine golden sand to catch his breath and looked up into the sky, it was starting to get dark. He had nowhere to go, was all alone and didn't know where to start looking for his family. He put his little head in his hands, what was he going to do and where would he start looking?

Feeling very lonely and sorry for himself he curled up in a ball under the stars, he just wanted the nightmare to end and be reunited with his family. A tear ran down his sweet cheek, poor Cheeko he did not deserve to be alone like this.

In the distance he could hear the faint thud thud, thud sound coming from the enormous tree house and the sound of the waves started to send him to sleep. Cheeko began to doze off and as he did so he thought he could hear the pitter patter of footsteps on the sand behind him, but it was pitch black and he could see nothing.

Suddenly he felt something cold and wet touch the back of his head, oh no it's starting to rain thought Cheeko, I have no shelter. Then he felt it again, it was as if something was sniffing him. Cheeko jumped up startled and turned around. Standing there in front of him was a four-legged animal with two ears, a long wagging tail, and a big pink tongue. Its fur was sand colour and it had a red collar around its neck.

"What are you? Why did you sniff me? Do you want to eat me?" cried Cheeko.

"No, no my dear friend, my name is Sandy, I am a dog. I can see that you look very sad and puzzled, so I thought you might need a friendly face."

"Oh well yes I do," said Cheeko. "You see my home has been destroyed and I have nowhere to live. I have been separated from my family and I need to find them."

"I will help you all I can," said Sandy. "I too was separated from my family when I was just a puppy. I did have a master who treated me very well, but one day my master never returned home and I have had to fend for myself ever since. Come with me to my shelter for the night, it is warm and dry and we will be safe."

"Thank you very much, that is very kind of you," replied Cheeko.

Sandy and Cheeko set off down the beach together until they reached a little cave like shelter, far away from all the strange two-legged creatures.

"This is where I call home, we will be safe here as I have lived here for a long time and no one has bothered me," said Sandy.

"Not even the horrible two-legged creatures?" asked Cheeko.

"Creatures?" said Sandy, she looked puzzled.

"You know, there are hundreds of them walking about everywhere, thinking they own the place and living in large tree houses. They destroyed my home and now I have been separated from my family."

"Oh you mean the people," said Sandy.

"People, what are people?" asked a puzzled Cheeko.

"They are also known as humans, they are not creatures. My master was a human, they are the masters of this island and other islands just like it and they are not tree houses they are hotels where people come and visit the island. Do not worry I will look after you and you are very welcome to stay here as long as you wish," said Sandy.

Sandy's home wasn't a very big shelter, it was more like a little den made out of rock, where the sea had worn it away and created a cave.

"Squeeze in here, there's enough room," said Sandy.

Cheeko and Sandy managed to squeeze into the little den and finally settled down for the night. Cheeko struggled to get to sleep as Sandy snored very loudly and her tail kept hitting him in the face. He also had to keep his eye on the sea, as it gushed right up to his little feet, just touching his toes. This made them very wet and a few times a large wave would roll in and almost wash him away.

It was a big relief when morning finally came and the sun poked its shiny head up on the horizon. Cheeko jumped up, just in time, as an enormous wave almost washed over him, phew that was close he thought.

Cheeko had had a long and restless night and all he could taste was salt, it tasted horrible. His neck was stiff as he had slept in a funny position to escape Sandy's tail and his toes were all wrinkly and shrivelled from getting too wet. Cheeko was not happy and not used to such difficult living conditions, he was used to swinging freely from the trees and having lots of space.

Sandy was still fast asleep and twitching as if she was dreaming, but Cheeko was wide awake and getting very hungry and could not wait any longer. He decided to give her a gentle nudge to wake her up and as he did so she gave a startled bark. Cheeko jumped in fright and hit his head on the roof of the cave.

"OWWW," he yelled.

"So sorry, you startled me, I had forgotten I had my little monkey friend staying with me," said Sandy.

"Please can we go and collect our breakfast, I am very hungry," whined Cheeko.

"I am afraid I have to rely on the good nature of the two-legged humans," said Sandy. "If they decide to give me food then I have breakfast, if not then I do not eat."

Cheeko was horrified, he was so used to just walking into the forest and taking his food whenever he was hungry. Now he had to beg for it, it was horrible, he couldn't believe what was happening to him.

"Come on, let us head off down to the beach and if we are lucky a kind human will give us our breakfast," said Sandy.

As the pair trundled down the beach they came across a fishing boat. Fisherman had taken it out to sea early that morning, in the hope of catching fish to sell at the local market. Sandy sat down by the side of the boat and whispered to Cheeko; "watch what I do and copy me."

Sandy gave out a little bark to get the fishermen's attention. Cheeko copied Sandy and gave out a high-pitched chatter. Sandy then rolled over onto her back and started to playfully roll about. Oh no, thought Cheeko, have I got to do that as well? sand will get all in my fur.

Sandy nudged him; "do it," she whispered. Cheeko did as he was told and rolled over onto his back and began wriggling in the sand.

"Look at those daft pair, we have a double act, a dog and a monkey," shouted one of the fishermen and they both started laughing. Then one of them threw a large fish towards Sandy.

Sandy jumped up, barked, grabbed the fish in her mouth and ran off. Cheeko not realising she had gone was still rolling around on his back looking rather silly. Hearing Sandy barking in the distance Cheeko quickly jumped up but was covered in sand from head to toe. He shook his little body from side to side, creating a mini sand storm, to get rid of the sand. Cheeko then scuttled off hastily towards Sandy, feeling rather stupid.

"You see, we have a lovely large fish for breakfast," said Sandy.

Cheeko just stared at the fish. "I have never eaten this before. I normally eat berries and fruit and drink fresh sweet coconut milk, not a slimy wriggling fish that smells like the sea."

Sandy gave a big sigh; "you might like it and fish is very good for you, we will take it home and share it."

Off they trundled, Sandy walking with the big fish in her mouth and Cheeko lagging behind. They arrived back home and Sandy began to tuck into the fish, throwing Cheeko a small piece. Very unwillingly he placed it in his mouth and began to chew it. The texture was very different from what he was used to, fruit was very soft and juicy, this was slightly tough and salty.

"Not bad I suppose, I will just have to get used to it," said Cheeko.

"Do not worry, we will try and find you some fruit, but for now you will have to share my fish," replied Sandy.

Over the next few weeks Sandy and Cheeko grew to be very close friends. They had even made friends with the two-legged creatures that Cheeko had feared. One human in particular called Junior used to save them food everyday; fresh fruit for Cheeko and meat or fish for Sandy. Junior was a waiter at the large tree house, or as Sandy called it hotel, and because of Junior's kindness Cheeko even began to think that the humans weren't so bad after all.

Cheeko's friendship with Sandy had helped him survive and Sandy was happy as she was no longer alone on the island, they had each found their soul mate.

Cheeko had not forgotten his family and when they went out for food he would look out for them. Although he was beginning to think that he might never see them again and that Sandy was now his new family. He promised himself that one day he would be reunited with them, as he really missed his little brothers' games and his lazy bossy sister.

Chapter 4

Calypso and Coconuts

One fine sunny day, after a long night of rain, Cheeko and Sandy arose quite late and had to hurry to try and catch Junior for their breakfast before he went home.

As they got closer to the hotel they could see a little boat, being driven by a human, had pulled up on the beach. It was quite a small boat, smaller than the fishing boats that Cheeko had seen before. It was blue with a white stripe all around it and had the words 'Calypso' painted on it in black. Cheeko sniffed the air, the boat gave off a horrible dirty smell.

Cheeko and Sandy quickly scurried along to catch Junior for their breakfast. Luckily he was still there and gave them a nice feast of fish and fruit, he even threw in a bit of steak for Sandy.

After they had finished they started to make their way back down to the beach to go home. In front of them they could see the human had got out of the boat, he was carrying a lot of square boards with colours on and was stacking them up against a wall. Cheeko and Sandy walked past him and as Cheeko did so he knocked a board over with his tail, leaving just one board stood against the wall.

Cheeko looked and suddenly gasped loudly with horror. For there to his amazement, right in front of him, were five monkeys identical to his family except they were all flat and stuck on a square board. They all had their own individual markings that only Cheeko would know. Cheeko shrieked again and started jumping up and down, making his high-pitched chatter sound.

"What on earth is the matter?" Calm down and tell me what is wrong," asked a concerned Sandy.

Cheeko could barely talk his little teeth were chattering together, he was in shock. "My family, my family," are the only words he could say.

"Where, where?" asked Sandy.

Cheeko just pointed towards the square object in front of them.

"My family, they have been squashed by the big yellow monster with the long arm and giant claw."

"No, no that is a painting," said Sandy. "The human is an artist, he paints things he has seen onto canvas and sells them to tourists. He is from another island and every so often he will come over to this island and sell his paintings. This could mean only one thing, your family are still safe and have probably escaped across the ocean to another island."

"What shall I do?" shrieked Cheeko.

"Leave it to me I will come up with a plan. For now we must go back to the cave, we will come back at the same time tomorrow," said Sandy.

The next day Cheeko and Sandy set off for their breakfast. Sandy had come up with a cunning plan to help Cheeko find his family again. They met Junior and ate their breakfast, keeping a beady eye out for the artist as they did so.

After they had finished they waited for the boat to come, but there was no sign of it. After hours and hours of waiting they decided to give up hope as by now it was late afternoon and so they started to make their way back home. Cheeko was so disappointed, especially after seeing the picture of his family. This made him even more determined to find them, for he knew they couldn't be too far away.

Cheeko and Sandy had walked back a fair distance along the beach and were nearly home. It was then that Cheeko thought he could smell the horrible dirty smell of the boat. He put his nose up in the air and took a deep breath in.

"I can smell it, I can smell Calypso," cried Cheeko.

"Don't be silly," said Sandy, "I cannot smell it, it must be your imagination."

"No, quick, let's run back down the beach," shouted an excited Cheeko.

"I fear Cheeko that you are dreaming. I have an excellent sense of smell and all I sense is the salty sea air and heat from the hot tropical sun," replied Sandy.

"No I can definitely smell it, please I beg you Sandy. If I am wrong I will eat fish for a week."

"Very well," agreed a reluctant Sandy.

They both ran back down the beach as quick as they could and upon turning a sharp corner there right in front of them was the little boat Calypso. It had just pulled up on the beach and Cheeko jumped in the air with joy.

"I told you, I told you," shrieked an excited Cheeko.

"Now we can put our plan into action," said Sandy, and they made their way towards the little boat.

The artist was getting out of his boat and was loaded up with even more paintings, he had been busy. Sandy followed him along the path towards the hotel. She caught a glimpse of one of his paintings and could see it looked like a big red bird. It had a big orange beak and beautiful blue and yellow feathers, the bird looked magnificent. Sandy had never seen a bird so exotic before and wondered where the human could have seen such a thing.

By this time the artist had stopped, put down his paintings and was talking to their friend Junior. Sandy stood behind them and turned around to look at Cheeko, she gave a little bark, this was Cheeko's signal to go.

The artist left his paintings at the hotel and started to head back towards his boat. Sandy immediately ran in front of him, blocking his path and barking very loudly.

Cheeko could hear Sandy barking and quickly jumped into the boat, but he didn't know what to do, how did he make it work? He didn't have time to think, he just grabbed hold of a long piece of string at one end of the boat and pulled it. On doing so it made a loud noise, the engine had started up and the boat began to move.

The boat was all over the place, going around and around in circles. Cheeko had to be quick as Sandy couldn't hold back the artist any longer and he was running towards the boat, shaking his fist.

Cheeko quickly grabbed a lever in the centre of the boat and it began to straighten up and move away from the beach, leaving Sandy behind. As he looked back Sandy was barking at him, "GO CHEEKO GO." The artist just stood on the edge of the beach in disbelief as Cheeko drove off into the distance.

Cheeko got the hang of driving the boat pretty quickly and was really proud of himself, but couldn't help feeling sad as he looked back and saw Sandy's small figure stood on the edge of the beach. For now though he had to concentrate on driving the boat and finding his family, promising himself that one day he would return for Sandy.

Cheeko's island slowly disappeared, becoming a small dot in the middle of the ocean. As he continued to drive the boat the sun beamed down on him and the waves gently bounced off the side; it was very very peaceful. Cheeko even started to enjoy himself, chugging along in the little boat as if he hadn't got a care in the world and feeling like a true captain of his ship.

Unfortunately his peace and quiet was about to come to an abrupt end when there was a sudden loud bang, the boat jerked forward and came to a complete stop, knocking Cheeko to the ground. He was horrified, what on earth had happened? Water began seeping into the boat and Cheeko started to panic, he wasn't a strong swimmer, monkeys weren't keen on water and it was coming in faster and faster.

The boat had hit rocks, ripping a hole in the bottom and was sinking, he would have to jump ship. Cheeko grabbed what he could from the boat, a bit of old rope and a wooden box and jumped into the sea. He was just in time as the boat started gurgling and cracking, it then turned upright and slowly sank to the bottom of the sea. Oh no, what shall he do now? He could end up anywhere, just drifting along for forever and a day.

For two days and two nights Cheeko drifted on his wooden box, hanging on for dear life as he battled large waves, with not a soul or a bit of land in sight. At night he could hear only strange noises coming from beneath him and he couldn't see a thing, everywhere was pitch black. The darkness was even worse than when he was in his forest tree house and by now he was at his wits end.

It was Cheeko's third day at sea and as dawn broke everything seemed calm, not a ripple or wave in sight. Cheeko was bobbing about peacefully on his box when his attention was drawn to faint splashing noises, but when he looked around he could see nothing. Then all of a sudden something jumped as quick as lightening in the air and disappeared back into the sea.

This jumping and splashing went on for a few minutes, but it was far too fast for Cheeko to see what it was. He could hear giggling and saw something shiny out of the corner of his eye. Quickly turning around, he saw what looked like a fish frantically flapping its fins and hovering above the surface of the sea. It was rather small, silvery blue in colour, with three dark blue stripes on its side and had a very cheeky grin.

"Greetings my friend, my name is Frisby. What is your name?"

"My name is Cheeko and I am very confused, are you a bird or a fish?

"I am a creature of the sea, not the sky, I am a flying fish. What brings you out this far in the ocean my furry friend? You do not look like you can swim or fly. Are you in a spot of bother?" asked Frisby.

"Yes I am. My family disappeared from our home and we have become separated. I was on my way to try and find them but my boat sank and I have been drifting at sea for three days," replied Cheeko.

"Fear not, I will call my troops and we will help you safely to shore. For all creatures must help one another in their hour of need," said Frisby.

Frisby then dipped his head into the sea, disappearing for a second, and came back up to the surface wearing a pair of flying goggles.

"Captain Frisby flying fish at your service, Sir." He then saluted Cheeko with his wing-like fin, gave out a sharp whistle and bellowed in a deep loud voice; "ATTENTION."

At precisely that moment out of the sea jumped a large shoal of flying fish. It was a spectacular sight; these silvery blue fish, with just one dark blue stripe, were flapping their fins and hovering above the sea, just like a flock of birds.

Captain Frisby shouted; "FISH MATES ON MY COMMAND PREPARE FOR OPERATION MONKEY RESCUE."

Cheeko was amazed, one minute he was talking to a delicate little flying fish, the next he had turned into a Sergeant Major, shouting drill commands to a troop of flying fish.

"FINS AT THE READY," shouted Captain Frisby.

On this command the fish pushed their flying fins straight back as if they were about to go into battle.

Captain Frisby shouted; "ABOUT TURN."

The flying fish lifted the rope out of the water with their mouths and hovered above the sea. Captain Frisby gave a loud whistle and the flying fish began to dip in and out of the waves, criss-crossing precisely over one another as they did so; eventually tying the rope around Cheeko's wooden box.

Once the rope was secure the flying fish began to pull Cheeko gently along on his box as if he was surfing. Captain Frisby was at the front of the troop shouting orders to his soldiers as they dipped in and out of the waves.

Sometimes the waves were quite big and went right over the top of Cheeko. He would reappear out of the surf holding onto the box for dear life, the salty sea splashing in his eyes and ears.

An extremely huge wave hit Cheeko's box causing him to fall off, he was being dragged from behind just holding onto the rope, he had to use all his strength to pull himself up. As he did he noticed a lovely yellow starfish hitching a ride, clinging onto the side of the box, it winked at Cheeko as he pulled himself back up.

After what seemed like hours, Cheeko eventually saw land and was pulled swiftly to shore. He was so grateful to his new friends, he would never have made it without them and who knows what would have become of him.

"Thank you," shouted Cheeko as he fell off his box onto the white sandy beach.

"Any time and good luck," shouted Captain Frisby. He then bellowed the final order to his troops; "AT EASE, DISSSMISSS."

The shoal of spectacular flying fish turned, saluted Cheeko and swam away, bouncing along like a handful of pebbles skimming across the surface of the ocean.

Cheeko brushed himself down, gathered himself together and stood and looked around. This island looked a lot bigger than his home, the sand was a lot softer and very white, as if someone had sprinkled icing sugar all around.

Dotted about on this beautiful fine sand were large shells, so large in fact Cheeko could almost fit inside and they were a lovely pink colour. The palm trees on the island looked like tall one-legged nodding giants with bushy hairdos and they towered along the shoreline. The sea seemed a lot rougher here, the waves were really tall and came crashing onto the shore.

Cheeko was very scared, who knows what dangers he was going to come across on his journey to find his family and they may not even be here. Taking a deep breath he decided to go clockwise around the island to see what he could find. It was very hot, the sun was beating down on him and his fur felt very salty and stiff from falling into the sea. He was also very hungry and thirsty and hoped he would find something tasty to eat.

Cheeko had been walking around the island for what seemed like an eternity. There wasn't a soul in sight, not even a humming bird or dragonfly, until he came upon a large spiral shaped shell sat alone on the beach. Cheeko bent down to investigate what it was and sniffed it. To his amazement it moved, just an inch, Cheeko jumped back, it moved again but this time a bit further.

Upon seeing it had no wings or legs, Cheeko turned the shell over, he was very curious. Kneeling down he pushed his head right into the shell to see what he could see, suddenly coming face to face with a large black beady eye.

Startled, Cheeko tried to pull his head out, he tugged and tugged with all his strength but it was no use his head was stuck. He stood up and started panicking, running along the beach trying to pull the shell off his head, all the time the black beady eye still staring right at him.

Something sharp pinched his nose; "AAHH," cried Cheeko, his cry echoing around the shell as if he were in a tunnel. With that whatever was inside the shell gave Cheeko's head a big push, squeezing it out.

Cheeko fell backwards and landed in the sand, bottom first and legs poking upwards. The shell bounced a short distance along the beach and as it stopped two large claws emerged from it, followed by two beady black eyes. It was a very large red crab and it was shouting angrily at Cheeko.

"DO NOT COME INTO FRANCOIS' HOUSE UNINVITED." The crab then scurried off down the beach waving its claws in the air.

Cheeko pulled himself out of the sand, shook his head and continued on his way.

Cheeko was getting rather tired after his ordeal and luckily a short distance down the beach he stumbled across a very large rock that was nicely situated under a palm tree, or as Cheeko called it, a nodding giant.

The rock was like a large mound, had very pretty squared patterns on it and smelt quite musty and salty. Cheeko decided to have a few minutes rest on the rock. It was so large that he was able to lie down and stretch out, he was so relaxed in fact he dozed off.

Cheeko hadn't been asleep for long when he suddenly awoke startled, for everything was swaying from side to side. Oh no thought Cheeko, I feel sea sick, I must have had too much sun. He quickly sat up and to his amazement he wasn't dizzy at all, the so-called rock was moving.

Cheeko was quite high up and as he looked down he saw the rock had four legs poking out, two either side of it and could also see a head at the front with a piece of dried dark green seaweed stuck to it.

"Excuse me," shouted Cheeko. There was no reply from the walking rock.

"EXCUSE ME," he shouted again, really loudly this time.

The rock stopped, looked up, looked to the left and then to the right.

"I'm up here, on your back," shouted Cheeko.

The walking rock turned around, gulped and said; "I do beg your pardon, I am a little bit deaf, for I am over a 100 years old. Who are you and where did you come from, did you fall from the sky?"

"I was having a rest from my long and tiring journey and I thought you were a large rock," said Cheeko.

"Let me introduce myself, my name is Dillbert the tortoise. A long journey you say, what is that all about?"

"I have come to your island in search of my family. I was separated from them when our home was invaded and destroyed by humans."

Dillbert gave a huge sigh; "aah the humans, just as I feared."

"What do you mean?" asked Cheeko.

"For many years my ancestors predicted that the creature known as the human would destroy our beautiful islands. They would build their homes and hotels on our land and chop down our rainforests, making it more and more difficult for us to live in our natural environment," said Dillbert.

"These actions will eventually wipe out whole species of animals making them extinct forever. We are totally helpless Cheeko, if man

39

chooses to invade our islands he will strip our forests bare. All wildlife will flee, our peace and harmony will disappear forever; our fresh sweet air with be polluted with his toxic fumes."

Cheeko just sat listening with his mouth wide open in horror. "That is exactly what happened to my home. It was invaded and my family have now disappeared, I am searching to find them."

"Then good luck to you Cheeko, I can offer you one piece of advice, never put all your trust in a stranger, always be on your guard."

With that Cheeko jumped off Dillbert's back and they said their goodbyes. Dillbert slowly plodded off into the distance and eventually disappeared out of sight.

By now it was early afternoon and Cheeko was very hungry. What if there were no other animals on the island only Dillbert? He was very old and ancient and could have outlived all the other animals, Cheeko would be stranded here forever all on his own.

With this scary thought Cheeko continued on his journey and in the distance a flicker of light suddenly caught his eye. Very carefully he followed it until he stumbled upon a little shack that stood all on its own, surrounded by tall nodding giants.

40

The shack was made of bright pink wood and had a white front door with a 'Home Sweet Home' sign hanging from it. There was a lovely smell coming from the shack that filled the air. Cheeko's tummy rumbled, he knew it would be very dangerous if he were to enter the shack and he didn't know who or what was in there, but he was so hungry and the smell was so good.

Deciding to take a peep through the window he pulled himself up onto a window box and hid amongst its pretty red flowers. Peeping through the window a huge bunch of bright yellow bananas caught his eye, they were the biggest he had ever seen and then his tummy really began to rumble.

Just one banana to fill my tummy thought Cheeko, no one will miss just one banana. The window was slightly open and Cheeko squeezed himself through it, the bananas were right in front of him.

Yet again curiosity getting the better of him, he decided to investigate the lovely smell and follow his nose. It led him into another room where a big stewing pot full of fresh vegetables was cooking on a stove. That smells really good thought Cheeko, but I must not hang around as it is far too dangerous to stay here. He had ventured too far into the shack and it was time to make a quick exit.

Cheeko turned around to leave, but as quick as a flash everything suddenly went dark. Cheeko could see nothing and was aware of a horrible musty smell that made him cough. He could feel something rough and prickly against his fur and something very close to him was breathing very loudly.

At first Cheeko thought someone had turned the lights out, he struggled and shrieked, but it was no use he was trapped. Someone had put him in a sack and tied the top with rope so he couldn't escape. Cheeko began making a distress signal in his high-pitched chatter, but there were no other monkeys there to save him. Soon getting exhausted with all the struggling and shrieking he decided to give up, there was no escape, he had been captured.

Cheeko was then carried in the sack and thrown into the air, hitting a hard surface as he landed. The ground then started to move for what seemed like hours. When it eventually stopped something picked Cheeko up and carried him. By this time he was very hot, itchy and frightened and could hardly breathe. Wondering what was to become of him his little teeth started to chatter in fear and his knees began to tremble.

Chapter 5

Little Wooden Shack Shack

Little did Cheeko know his ordeal had only just begun. The rope from around the top of the sack was untied and he was lifted out by two very large hands, belonging to a human. He was then pushed into a tiny cage that was hanging down from the ceiling. The door slammed shut on the cage and it was locked by a big gold key that was then taken away by Cheeko's captor.

The cage was very rusty and there was hardly any room to stand up, never mind swing about. There was a little bit of dirty water and a small piece of rotten fruit in the bottom of the cage.

Cheeko looked around, he was inside another shack similar to the pink one with the bright yellow bananas. This time there was hardly any light as the shutters on the windows were closed, letting only a little bit of sunshine through. It was very cluttered and untidy and the smell from the shack was old and stale, with a smoky haze filling the room.

Cheeko put his head in his hands in disbelief, he was having the worst time of his life. Had the same thing happened to his family?

The next morning the human threw a few scraps of food into Cheeko's cage. This happened at the same time everyday and then the human would leave and not return until late at night or early morning. Sometimes he disappeared for days, leaving poor Cheeko with no food at all until he returned.

The days were very long and the nights even longer for Cheeko who had nothing to do but just stare and think.

The weeks past by and Cheeko got sadder and sadder. He began to think he would never see his family again and feared he would be sad forever, locked up in this horrible cage. No more swinging from the trees or running through the forest, laughing and giggling with his

brothers. His freedom had been snatched away from him, gone forever.

Cheeko was feeling really sorry for himself when the front door of the shack flung open and in charged the human carrying another sack. Whatever was inside was wriggling frantically trying to get out and making loud squawking sounds.

The human tipped the sack upside down and out fell what looked like a large bright red bird with lovely blue and yellow feathers and a big orange beak. It was making a really high-pitched sound and frantically flapping its wings trying to fly away. The large bird was then pushed into a tiny cage, the door slammed shut and locked with the same large gold key. The human then disappeared from sight.

Cheeko had never seen such a fine looking bird, it was very beautiful and elegant. It began to preen its ruffled feathers, as they were sticking up all over the place after the frantic struggle.

"Hello, are you alright?" said Cheeko.

"Yes," squawked the bird."

"You are a beautiful looking bird I haven't seen anything like you before. Let me introduce myself my name is Cheeko. What is your name?"

"I am a Macaw parrot and my name is Loretta. I lived hundreds of miles away, but I was captured in a large net along with other parrots. My captors then sent me on a long journey and this is where I have ended up. What happened to you, how did you end up here?"

"I came to this island to try and find my family. You see the humans invaded my old home, destroyed our rainforest and all the animals have fled. I have been separated from my family and I was searching for them when I became captured," said Cheeko.

"I too used to live high up in the trees along with my five brothers and six sisters," replied the parrot. "We were a spectacular sight displaying our beautiful colours, until one day two of my brothers and one sister disappeared. We do not know what became of them, my parents used to go out at night calling for them. The whisper through the trees was they had been captured and taken a long way away from home, never to be seen again. Now the same has happened to me."

"Oh that is so sad, we have got to get out of here. I will not spend the rest of my life in this cage away from my family," said Cheeko.

The parrot replied; "I would like my freedom back too, we will have to try and escape."

Over the next few weeks Loretta and Cheeko became firm friends, keeping one another's spirits up. The food they were given was very poor, they were only given water twice a week and it was also very hot and stuffy inside the shack.

Cheeko could barely stand upright in the cage as it was so small and his long curly tail dangled down, touching the floor. Loretta was also very cramped and couldn't stretch out her beautiful large wings to flap them about.

Unfortunately events took a turn for the worst for Cheeko. Late one hot sticky night he was curled up in a tight little ball trying to get some sleep, his tail dangling down and touching the floor.

The human arrived back at the shack and opened the door, as he walked past Cheeko he tripped on his dangling tail and went flying through the air, landing with a loud thud as he hit the deck. Cheeko jumped up startled as the human pulled his tail whilst falling to the floor. The human was out cold and didn't move a muscle.

Cheeko looked up and could see the large gold key had come out of the human's pocket and was spinning in the air. Cheeko and Loretta both had their eyes fixed firmly on it as it came back towards the ground in slow motion, landing right in front of Loretta's cage. Could this be their chance to escape? Cheeko and Loretta looked at one another and couldn't believe their luck.

"We must try and reach the gold key so we can escape, it is our only hope, but we haven't got long, the human could wake at any time," said Loretta.

Cheeko began to move his long tail across the floor, trying to grab hold of the key, but it was just too far away. Loretta then tried to reach it with her wings and after a long stretch managed to push it further towards Cheeko. This time he could reach and he pulled it towards him with his long green tail, then grabbed it and quickly undid his cage.

Cheeko ran over to Loretta's cage to free her, but as he did so he caught a glass of water with his tail, knocking it over onto the human's face.

"AAAH," shouted the human, who sat up very quickly, grabbing Cheeko's tail with his big hands. Cheeko shrieked in shock and tried to wriggle free from the human's grasp, but it was no use, he was too strong for poor Cheeko. The human scooped him up and whisked him away to another part of the shack, well away from Loretta.

Cheeko was thrown into another room, even more horrific than where he was before. There was no light at all and it smelt very musty, making him sneeze. The human snapped something cold onto Cheeko's leg and then left the room, slamming the door behind him in anger.

Cheeko was left all alone in the dark with no food or water at all. There wasn't even a window, just a little peephole in the wall of the wooden shack, where a streak of sunshine was able to creep through.

47

Cheeko went over to take a look through it, but felt something really heavy on his leg, he could barely lift it and bent down to touch his leg. To his horror there was a chain clasped tightly around his little ankle and it was attached to the middle of the floor, so he could only move around slightly.

Cheeko managed to make his way towards the peephole, dragging his chained leg behind him, but the chain was too short and yanked him backwards, not letting him go any further.

Cheeko leaned forwards and supported himself by putting his hands on the wall of the shack. He was then able to peep through the hole and to his delight he could see the greenery of trees; this was a very welcome sight for Cheeko.

There was no way he could escape at all now and poor Loretta was all on her own too, what would become of her? At least when they were together they used to keep each other's spirits up, now they were separated and Cheeko had been thrown into a worse place than before.

Chapter 6

Peepo

Cheeko was sat all alone in the dark, feeling very sad and lonely, when suddenly he was startled as a flap in the door opened. A large familiar hand angrily pushed food and water through it.

Cheeko went over and could just about reach it, his chain was too short and he really had to stretch to get it. It wasn't very nice food at all, it was soggy and horrible. The room was so dark he couldn't even see what he was eating and the water tasted very salty.

The days went slowly by and Cheeko could hear the birds singing and the sound of monkeys in the distance calling one another. This could mean only one thing, he wasn't far from a rainforest.

Cheeko longed to be back in the wild and smell proper fresh air and swing amongst the trees, eating fresh fruit. Lying there at night he would listen to the rain falling and to pass the time he would count raindrops as they hit the shack's tin roof.

To amuse himself in the day Cheeko would look through the peephole, just to get a glimpse of the forest and life outside. It was the highlight of his day and he would dream he was swinging through the trees, playing with his brothers. He could hear his mother calling out to him for his delicious fruit and sweet coconut milk breakfast.

One particular day Cheeko was looking through the peephole and he had drifted off daydreaming about collecting dragonflies down at the mangrove pond. Suddenly he saw a large shadow in the shape of a monkey walk past. It must be his imagination he thought and he carried on daydreaming, taking no notice.

The next day he was peeping through the hole as usual, trying to breathe in some fresh air, when again it seemed like a shadow of a monkey had walked past very slowly.

Cheeko couldn't believe it and in a sweet little voice he tried to attract its attention and quietly shouted; "help," being careful not to alert his captor. The shadow stopped and looked back in Cheeko's direction. Cheeko tried again in a loudish whisper; "please help me."

The shadow began to walk towards him and to Cheeko's delight he could see it was another monkey, very different to Cheeko, but it definitely was a monkey. It was bigger with short dark fur, not green at all and it had no tail, very long arms and big flat feet.

The monkey got closer and Cheeko was dazzled by a beautiful glistening silver shell, tied with string around its neck. As the sunlight caught the shell glorious colours of the rainbow bounced off it and shone all around.

The monkey stopped just outside Cheeko's peephole. It looked around, scratched its head and carried on walking past. Cheeko was horrified the monkey had gone, he was so desperate to escape and his lifeline had just walked away. All he could do was pray the monkey would return tomorrow.

After a long night, morning came and the sun beamed its ray of light through the peephole. Cheeko jumped up and ran towards it, forgetting about his chain for a second in his excitement, but it pulled him back sharply with a jolt. Cheeko picked himself up and moved over to the hole, eagerly awaiting the monkey's return.

After waiting patiently for a few hours sure enough the monkey began to walk towards Cheeko.

"Help me," cried Cheeko.

His cry was a bit louder this time as he wasn't about to let the monkey go past without hearing him. The monkey looked straight at Cheeko's peeping eye and stopped, rubbed his own eyes and carried on walking. Cheeko again tried to attract its attention.

"PLEASE, PLEASE HELP ME," shouted Cheeko in a fairly loud voice, as he was now getting very desperate to attract the monkey's attention. This time the monkey stopped, turned around and came back to where Cheeko's large brown sad eye was peeping through the hole. Cheeko's face was pressed so hard against the hole that his long eyelashes were poking out of it.

"What on earth is going on, are you playing tricks on me whatever you are?" said the monkey in a deep rough voice.

"No, no I am very sorry to bother you. I am a little green monkey from a neighbouring island," replied Cheeko.

"Then what are you doing in there little green monkey?"

"Well I have been captured and thrown into this room by a human who has chained me to the middle of the floor, so I cannot escape. I had been searching for my family as we have been separated. Our island home has been invaded and destroyed by humans, gone forever. They have built a hotel where my family home once stood, our peace and harmony gone forever."

"Tell me no more, this must be a horror story," screeched the monkey.

"No, no this is all very true," insisted Cheeko.

By now the monkey had started to believe Cheeko as he knew animals did not tell tales to one another. He was absolutely horrified that any animal could be treated in such a way.

"What is your name?" enquired the monkey.

"My name is Cheeko, what is your name?"

"Well my proper name is Tangakwunua, I am a Bonobo monkey, but you can call me Tanga-Tanga."

"I have never seen a monkey like you before," said Cheeko.

"That is because I am a rare species of monkey," replied Tanga-Tanga.

"Not a chimp then?" asked Cheeko.

"I most certainly am not, I am very special," said Tanga-Tanga.

"Do you like fresh juicy berries and large yellow bananas?" asked Cheeko.

"I most certainly do. Does the human feed you juicy berries and bananas?" asked Tanga-Tanga.

"No I am fed horrible soggy food that I cannot even see to eat as it is so dark in here," replied Cheeko.

"I will go and fetch you bananas and push them through your peeping hole my friend. Don't despair I will be back soon," said Tanga-Tanga.

"Oh thank you so much, I am so hungry and I would be very grateful," said Cheeko.

Tanga-Tanga disappeared out of sight, singing a little tune as he went. Cheeko sat down on the floor, he had been waiting for the monkey for a long time and his legs were hurting him.

Time went on and it started to get dark, Cheeko began to think Tanga-Tanga had disappeared forever. After all why should he help Cheeko? He didn't know him and probably had his own family to look after. He was also a totally different monkey species than Cheeko. Why would a rare cool dude of a monkey help an ordinary little green monkey?

Cheeko sat in the middle of the floor with his knees up to his chin feeling sorry for himself. Tanga-Tanga was his only hope and it looked like his hopes had been dashed. The chain was starting to irritate his ankle and was becoming very itchy, he was even losing his fur where it had rubbed him.

Cheeko was just about to curl up and cry himself to sleep, as he had by now given up on Tanga-Tanga, when suddenly he heard a loud deep grunt. He crawled over to the peephole and there to his delight Tanga-Tanga had kept his word and returned. Cheeko screeched excitedly at the thought of lovely fresh food.

"Oh thank you for helping me Tanga-Tanga."

"I am a monkey of my word, but remember I am a rare species and a very laid back monkey. Your today is Tanga-Tanga's tomorrow."

Tanga-Tanga then started to push banana through the peephole. By the time he had squoze it through, it was more like mush but Cheeko didn't mind, for by now he was really hungry and was very grateful for any food he could get.

Over the next few days Tanga-Tanga and Cheeko became buddies. Tanga-Tanga would visit Cheeko once a day to bring him food and he would lift Cheeko's spirits when he was feeling down. Tanga-Tanga was a lively, bubbly character always thinking positive, never negative.

One day Tanga-Tanga said to Cheeko; "you cannot stay here forever, this is no place for a wild fun loving monkey."

"I fear I will be trapped here forever Tanga-Tanga, never to see my family again. I will grow old and grey in this dungeon. I will never swing through the trees or play my favourite games with my brothers ever again."

"We will have none of that talk. You must believe in your dreams Cheeko, for mixed with a sprinkling of monkey magic your dreams will come true."

"I dream of being with my family, playing and being happy," said Cheeko.

"All I will say is; follow your dreams and you will surely find your pot of gold at the end of the rainbow. Never give up Cheeko," insisted Tanga-Tanga.

"Gold, I don't want gold, I want my family back," said Cheeko.

Tanga-Tanga just winked at him. "You will see," he said with a cunning smile.

"What shall we do Tanga-Tanga? I have a friend who is also captured inside this shack. Her name is Loretta, she is a beautiful parrot, we must escape so we can be free again to roam the forest and eat fresh fruit."

"What kind of monkey is a parrot, it surely cannot be as rare as a Bonobo monkey?" asked Tanga-Tanga.

Cheeko began to laugh; "she is not a monkey, a parrot is a beautiful bird of different colours, red, yellow, blue and white. She has large wings and can fly through the trees."

"Never fear Tanga-Tanga is here, I will get you out, leave it to me," and he turned and disappeared into the trees.

It had been a very exhausting few days for Cheeko and he was now very full from his first decent meal in weeks. Cheeko decided to get some sleep and his mind began to think about Loretta, what had become of her? He wondered if his family were safe and happy and if he would ever see them again.

Eventually he drifted off to sleep and started to dream about rainbows, gold and the good times when he used to play with his brothers. He so missed playing his favourite game of race the dragonfly and longed to try and catch them again on the mangrove pond. All night long Cheeko dreamt of being free and the fun he used to have with his family.

Chapter 7

The Great Escape

Morning arrived and Cheeko awoke with a yawn and a stretch. For a moment he had forgotten where he was and thought he was still in his dream, until he moved his leg and felt the chain attached to it. His heart sank, he was still trapped in the shack with no way of escaping.

Crawling over to the peephole he peeped through hoping to see Tanga-Tanga. Instead he got an awful shock, he looked away, rubbed his eyes and took another look, there walking towards him was the artist. Cheeko quickly came away and hid up the corner, just in case he had seen his peeping eye. He couldn't believe it, the artist was on the island too.

Does this mean Cheeko's family are on this island? His little heart began to race, I really must get out of here he thought, what if he had captured his family?

Cheeko calmed himself down and sat waiting and hoping Tanga-Tanga would return. The minutes turned into hours and there was still no sign of him.

As night began to fall, the ray of sunshine that beamed through the peephole began to disappear, Cheeko was again in darkness. It had been a very long day waiting for Tanga-Tanga to return and Cheeko felt it was going to be an even longer night. He was very sad and had given up all hope of ever being free again and seeing Tanga-Tanga.

It started to rain heavily and to pass the time Cheeko began to count the raindrops as they hit the roof. Cheeko had just counted three hundred raindrops when he was suddenly interrupted by a loud thud which made him jump.

Cheeko could hear very loud squawking, banging and clattering, as if things were being knocked over and thrown about. This kafuffle went on for a few seconds, then it all went very quiet and there was complete silence.

The door then suddenly flung open, Cheeko was terrified for he could just see a figure standing in the doorway, it was very dark and he couldn't make out what it was.

Frightened for his life his legs began to shake and the chain around his ankle clanked as his knees knocked. Putting his hands in front of his eyes he couldn't bear to look and then a deep voice bellowed out; "are you going to sit there all day?"

Cheeko peeped through his fingers; "Tanga-Tanga is that you?"

"Yes of course, never fear Tanga-Tanga is here."

Cheeko looked up and there was Tanga-Tanga. The room immediately lit up with all colours of the rainbow as Tanga-Tanga's necklace glistened in the darkness. He was stood there swinging the big gold key on his finger as if he were spinning a basketball.

Something was perched on Tanga-Tanga's shoulder but Cheeko couldn't quite see what it was. Rubbing his eyes, he took a closer look and to his amazement it was his parrot friend.

"Loretta are you okay?" Cheeko shrieked in delight.

"Yes, no thanks to this baboon, it nearly gave me the fright of my life."

"Firstly I am not a baboon, I am a rare Bonobo monkey and I am very cool and secondly I have saved your life and this is all the thanks I get."

"Ignore her she doesn't mean it, she can be very grumpy," said Cheeko and with that Loretta squawked very loudly.

"That was in my ear you crazy canary, you nearly deafened me," said Tanga-Tanga.

"Stop it you two, will you please get this horrible chain off my leg."

Tanga-Tanga then walked over to Cheeko with the gold key and undid the rusty chain that was attached around his ankle. Cheeko gave it a quick rub and jumped up.

"Quick let's get out of here before we are all captured," cried an anxious Cheeko.

Tanga-Tanga led the way through the shack. There was furniture and cutlery all over the floor, it looked like a hurricane had hit and there was no sign of the human.

"What on earth happened here?" enquired Cheeko.

"Let's just say the hurricane season came early," replied Tanga-Tanga.

Tanga-Tanga then opened the front door, letting in daylight. For a second Cheeko and Loretta were blinded by the sun, they hadn't seen proper daylight for weeks.

"Aah it is so bright it hurts my eyes," said Cheeko. Loretta covered her eyes with her wing as she sat on Cheeko's shoulder.

Cheeko stood in the big open space, stretched his arms and legs and sniffed the fresh sweet air. The tropical breeze gently blowing away the musty smell from his fur. It was so good to be free again and see the greenery of the trees and the blueness of the sky. Turning around he took one last look at the horrible prison shack.

"Follow me, I will lead you away from danger," said Tanga-Tanga.

He led them along a windy trail that was hidden amongst trees and bushes, until he stopped sharply.

"This is as far as I can take you my friends. Follow your monkey instincts and they will lead you to your pot of gold at the end of the rainbow."

"Thank you so much for everything," said Cheeko.

"You're welcome my little monkey friend, here take my shell, it will bring you good luck and keep evil away. When you are in trouble hold onto the shell and say to yourself; never fear Tanga-Tanga is here!"

"No, no I couldn't possibly take your shell, you have done enough already," said Cheeko.

"Take it you daft little green monkey and be safe. You will need it travelling with that grumpy old bird."

"Thank you, I will never forget you Tanga-Tanga the rare Bonobo monkey."

With that Tanga-Tanga turned around and walked away. As he disappeared out of sight they could hear him shouting; "remember Cheeko, follow your dreams and what you seek you shall find."

Cheeko put the shell around his neck; "he is one cool dude Loretta," who just squawked back, flapping her wings. She clearly wasn't impressed.

"It's just you and me now Loretta, I don't know where we are going, or what we shall find. Follow your dreams says Tanga-Tanga, but how do you know which way to go?"

"Silly dreams," squawked Loretta, still perched on Cheeko's shoulder.

Chapter 8

A Sprinkling of Monkey Magic

Cheeko and Loretta carried on following the windy trail until it began to split into two directions, one to the left and one to the right. Seeing two tall mountain peaks in the distance between the trees, Cheeko decided that they would go left and aim for the mountains.

A small speck of fluorescent light suddenly caught Cheeko's eye, disappearing into a puff of sparkling crystals as Cheeko walked past it. Rubbing his eyes Cheeko thought he must have been staring at the sun for too long and continued on his way.

After they had been travelling quite a while the trail disappeared and they started to venture into thick forest. It was by now late afternoon and Cheeko decided it was time to settle down before night-time fell. They continued until they came across an opening in the forest where the trees were not so thick, this was an ideal place to make a fire.

Cheeko perched Loretta safely on a branch so he could build his fire in peace. He began to gather bits of branches, laid them in a pile and then twizelled two sticks together to create a spark. The branches eventually ignited, making a brilliant fire. This would keep predators away at night and also keep them warm.

Loretta flew down from the branch and joined Cheeko around the fire. It was dark by now, the temperature had dropped and it was getting quite cold. Cheeko and Loretta huddled together and settled down for the night. Cheeko was so glad he wasn't on his own in the forest, it brought back a few scary memories of when he was living in his tree house.

Eventually they both dropped off to sleep and Cheeko began dreaming that Tanga-Tanga was stood at the end of a rainbow chanting; 'follow your dreams Cheeko, follow your dreams.'

In the middle of his dream Cheeko was awoken by a sudden cold splat hitting his head, he jumped up startled. A large raindrop had landed on his forehead, it was pouring down with rain and the fire had gone out, Cheeko quickly woke Loretta.

"We must hide under a tree for safety and shelter," said Cheeko.

They both found a large tree with bushy branches to shelter under and moved just in time before it started to thunder really loudly, echoing through the night. There then followed a large bolt of lightening, striking right in front of them, cracking very loudly as it hit the ground.

Cheeko looked and to his horror it had struck on the exact spot where they had been sleeping, leaving a large burn mark. Cheeko and Loretta were very shocked and continued to shelter under the tree in case lightening struck again.

Looking up Cheeko saw a large moon, with a big round face, light up the sky. There was a bright fluorescent speck on the tree trunk just above his head, disappearing into a puff of sparkling crystals, like a sparkler. Cheeko was very puzzled by this as it was dark and so he could not have been staring at the sun for too long. He decided to get some sleep in case his tired eyes were playing tricks on him.

By the time morning came the storm had past over and all seemed calm. Cheeko arose early for breakfast and went on a little walk to see what he could find. He spotted a large river that ran just to the side of them and decided to go and see if he could catch a fish for breakfast.

Making his way down to the edge of the river he could clearly see shoals of brown speckled fish that were jumping in the air and landing straight back in the water. Loretta would love a nice bit of fish he thought.

Cheeko gently waded into the river, just up to his ankles, as he was frightened of water. Crouching down he very quietly waited patiently for a fish to swim close and jump out of the water.

Eventually a brown fish with a large mouth swam over to where Cheeko was eagerly waiting and as it hurled itself out of the water Cheeko jumped up and put his hands out to catch it. There was an almighty splash and Cheeko belly flopped back into the water missing the fish. He again took up his crouched position and soon enough another fish swam along, jumping in the air.

This time Cheeko's timing was perfect, as he jumped he put his hands out and caught the fish's tail, holding tightly onto it as it wriggled frantically. There was a huge splash as they both crash landed into the water and Cheeko dragged the fish onto the river bank.

He was really pleased with himself and skipped back to camp with the fish breakfast. As he approached he could see Loretta was looking quite grumpy.

"This is no time for splashing about and having fun," she squawked.

"I know Loretta, I have caught you a nice fish for your breakfast, let us share it."

They both tucked into the fish, Cheeko thought it was quite nice and it didn't taste half as bad this time.

After breakfast they set off on their journey, following Cheeko's monkey instincts towards the mountains. Because of the thickness of the trees they could not see the two mountain peaks and they hoped they were heading in the right direction.

Cheeko started to get quite worried about his eyesight, for again he saw the small fluorescent speck of light. It seemed to disappear into a puff of sparkling crystals as soon as Cheeko caught sight of it.

Rubbing his eyes again he carried on following his monkey instincts, but he was getting nowhere as everywhere they turned the large river surrounded them. It was a very wide river and they did not want to have to cross it, for Cheeko could not swim very well and Loretta could not fly very far.

Making their way through the dense forest, Cheeko spotted a clearing just ahead and bright sunshine beaming through the trees. They followed the clearing, but again it led them to the large river.

"Oh no, everywhere we turn we are surrounded by this river," complained Cheeko; but then something stunning caught his eye.

Cheeko looked up and gasped in amazement for he could see the two mountain peaks, but they were not alone, for in-between them a beautiful multi-coloured rainbow had appeared. Cheeko couldn't believe it and he looked down at his shell and held it tightly.

"Look Loretta a rainbow, perhaps Tanga-Tanga was right and I will find what I am looking for at the end of the rainbow." Loretta squawked as usual and was no help at all.

"We must continue to follow the rainbow," shrieked Cheeko.

Unfortunately for Cheeko and Loretta there was one big problem, the large river that lay between them.

"We are going to have to cross the river that surrounds the forest otherwise we will be going around in circles forever. You fly across first Loretta and I will follow you," said Cheeko.

Loretta flapped her large wings for it was quite a while since she had flown any distance. She could not fly too far because her wings had been clipped by her captor so she couldn't escape.

"Good luck Loretta, you can do it," shouted Cheeko and off she flew just hovering above the water's surface.

At first she looked a bit shaky, as if she was going to hit the water. Eventually she made it across to the other side and gave out a loud squawk as she landed.

My turn now thought Cheeko and he put his toe into the water. It was so cold he didn't like it at all, but the thought of finding his family spurred him on.

Gradually he put both feet in, held his arms up in the air so they wouldn't get wet and began to wade across. The river got deeper and deeper the further he went, until he could touch the bottom no longer. Cheeko began splashing loudly as he frantically tried to move his arms and legs to swim across.

With all this splashing going on in the river, Cheeko didn't realise he was attracting attention from below the water's surface. This was a dangerous area for little monkeys to be in, for large crocodiles lay in wait to catch their lunch. Two large beady eyes had been watching his little arms and legs paddle and splash about. They were slowly and cunningly moving closer and closer to Cheeko.

Loretta had spotted the two eyes gliding on the surface of the water and was frantically trying to warn Cheeko by squawking loudly at him. Cheeko thought she was just moaning at him or trying to encourage him, he wasn't sure which and was far too busy trying to stop the strong current from sweeping him away down the river. At one point Loretta couldn't bear to look and covered her eyes with her wing.

The other side of the riverbank was in sight, he didn't have far to go. Then disaster struck, a strong under-current gripped hold of Cheeko and whisked him down the river, he wasn't strong enough to fight it and was helpless. Loretta frantically flapped her wings and made loud squawking noises at Cheeko, but all she could do was watch as he was swept away down the river.

Cheeko knew he could do nothing and shouted back to Loretta; "see you at the end of the rainbow," and with that he was out of sight. The current swept Cheeko close to the edge of the riverbank, where he managed to grab hold of a tree root and cling on for dear life, the current still trying to force him down the river.

Cheeko didn't just have the current to worry about, for the two beady eyes had been following him. While Cheeko was trying to hold onto the tree's root the crocodile was eyeing him up, for he looked very tasty. Cheeko was unaware that he was on the crocodile's lunch menu.

The crocodile was now right behind him and suddenly shot out of the water, its long jaws and gigantic teeth ready to strike. Just in time the tree root snapped and broke away from the riverbank sending Cheeko hurtling down the river. The crocodile's jaws missing him by a whisker, leaving it with a mouthful of branches and roots instead of a tasty monkey. Cheeko was now being swept away still holding onto the broken root in his hand and was really starting to panic, where would he end up?

As Cheeko was swept along, he looked ahead of him and could see the river disappearing over the edge of a magnificent waterfall. Cheeko frantically tried to swim against the current, moving his little arms and legs faster and faster against it, but it was still no good and he could see the edge of the waterfall getting closer and closer.

Remembering his shell necklace and what Tanga-Tanga had said to him, he took hold of it and thought to himself; 'never fear Tanga-Tanga is here,' but nothing happened.

Cheeko was running out of time, soon it would be too late and he would be falling over the edge of the waterfall. He tried again; 'never fear Tanga-Tanga is here,' again nothing happened.

It was too late Cheeko went right over the waterfall and was in mid air, falling quickly. His arms and legs were flapping as if he was riding an invisible bicycle; "AAAHHH," he yelled as he fell. In sheer desperation he grabbed his shell shouting loudly; "never fear Tanga-Tanga is here," and within a split second something grabbed him by the shoulders, just in the nick of time.

Cheeko looked up and saw a gigantic bird holding onto him. It was grey in colour and had a long orange beak with a big pouch underneath it. That looks like a pelican thought Cheeko, I have seen those before, near the sea, they hold lots of fish in their pouchy beaks.

Cheeko couldn't believe it, he looked down and began to admire the view. They were quite high up and Cheeko could see the tops of the trees in the forest and the river running all around it. In the distance he could see the mountains with the rainbow in-between and something glistening on top of one of them.

The bird then started to slowly glide down, Cheeko had no idea where it was taking him. It gradually got lower and lower and Cheeko could see that they were heading for a lagoon surrounded by trees. Just as Cheeko's legs were dangling above the water's surface the bird let go of him.

Cheeko splashed into the water and sank like a rock towards the bottom of the lagoon, oh no he was in trouble again. He was frantically moving his arms and legs, but nothing happened and he carried on sinking. Quickly grabbing hold of his shell he shouted; "never fear Tanga-Tanga is here," but only bubbles came out of his mouth.

Cheeko hit the seabed with a thud and as he did so the ground began to move and a cloud of sand appeared all around him. As it cleared Cheeko realised a sea turtle had come to his rescue and was carrying him through the water whilst he held onto its back. To Cheeko's amazement he could now breathe under water and as if by magic he was no longer spurting out bubbles.

"Wow this is great, look at the fabulous view," he shouted.

Cheeko could see beautiful coloured fish, yellow with black stripes, red ones, bright blue ones, orange ones, all colours you can think of. Bright pink crabs scurried along the bottom, sea horses swam past as if galloping in a race and dolphins were leaping and playing all around them.

There were beautiful coral reefs on the seabed swaying from side to side, all amazingly colourful, it was like an underwater garden. The sea was so much alive with lots of different creatures.

The sea turtle carried on until they came upon a very dark area that got darker as they swam towards it. As Cheeko looked up in front of him he saw a large ship lying still on the bottom of the sea. It was a shipwreck and was very spooky as it towered above them and shoals of fish swam in and out of the ship's windows.

Cheeko could see a lot of beady eyes looking back at them from different parts of the shipwreck and it was covered in seaweed and barnacles. A lot of sea creatures had made this their home.

The sea turtle then swam past the wreck, as he did so it got gloomier and gloomier. There were hardly any fish swimming around, only dark horrible looking fish, not brightly coloured.

All the coral reefs were black and shrivelled up, they weren't swaying from side to side. Cheeko could see a carpet of dead fish lined the bottom of the sea, it was like a graveyard. He gasped in horror at the sight of it.

The sea turtle stopped and turned to Cheeko; "shocking isn't it Cheeko? This is all because humans have wrecked our lovely ocean by dumping their pollution into our underwater garden and have ripped out our beautiful coral reefs to sell to holidaymakers. This area is completely dead, no fish swim past the shipwreck. If all our ocean ends up like this, it will be the end for us all."

"Oh my," said Cheeko. "It is bad enough the land being destroyed, never mind the ocean as well. Please tell me your name, beautiful creature of the sea?"

"My name is Scoot."

"Well Scoot I fear for you and all the other sea creatures. I am horrified at what devastation has been caused to your home."

"I think we have seen enough," said Scoot and with that he began to swim away from the dark side of the sea.

"Hold on tight," shouted Scoot and he started to head very quickly towards the surface. Cheeko held on as tight as he could and they broke the water's surface and came up with a splash. Scoot swam over to the water's edge to let Cheeko climb off his back.

"Thank you so much for showing me your underwater garden," said Cheeko.

"It is my pleasure. The beautiful side of the ocean may not exist in the future, at least you now know how beautiful it really is. Good luck with your journey Cheeko."

"By the way how do you know my name?" shouted a puzzled Cheeko.

"A sprinkling of monkey magic," shouted Scoot and with that his head disappeared under the water and he had gone.

Cheeko shook himself dry and looked up, he could just see the two mountain peaks, but to his horror the rainbow was fading with only half of it left. Oh no thought Cheeko does this mean my dreams are fading too? If I don't hurry the rainbow could soon disappear forever and my dreams will never come true.

Chapter 9

The End of the Rainbow

Cheeko had no time to waste, he had to reach the end of the rainbow fast before his dream disappeared forever. His monkey instincts told him the quickest way to reach his destiny would be to swing through the trees. It would be safe up there and nothing could stand in his way.

Cheeko began to climb a huge tree, meeting a lizard on his way up. It was quite a large brown lizard with black stripes around its skin and a very long tail that swished behind it.

The lizard had its eye on a rather juicy looking insect, who was unaware it was about to become lunch. The lizard stood quite still while it eyed up its prey. Not even its eyes moved, until it made a sudden jerk forward, rolled out its long pink tongue, grabbed the insect, and rolled it back into its mouth. Looking really pleased with itself it scurried back down the tree.

Cheeko eventually reached the top of the tree and started to swing amongst the treetops. This is what he loved to do, feeling free swinging amongst the trees. He had really missed it and never wanted to be trapped ever again.

It was now starting to get dark so he decided to spend the night in the treetops. Whilst he rested amongst the leafy branches his thoughts turned to Loretta; he didn't know where she was, or if she was okay. She couldn't fly properly, who knows what had become of her in the forest. Eventually Cheeko dozed off with Loretta in his thoughts.

Cheeko arose quite early the next morning and ate juicy berries for his breakfast and set about his journey. The rainbow was still in sight, but he could see that it had faded a little more so he had to be quick to reach it in time.

Cheeko carried on his journey, swinging merrily through the trees, minding his own business. Not paying too much attention to what he was doing, he made a silly monkey mistake and missed the next branch.

Cheeko began spinning and crashing towards the ground, hitting branches as he fell. On his way down he shouted; "never fear Tanga-Tanga is here," but it was too late and he hit a large ant's nest on the ground. It was about a foot high and luckily for Cheeko it had made a soft landing for him.

Cheeko quickly stood up and was covered in large ants, so big in fact they looked like they had muscles. Cheeko didn't mind too much though as he was quite partial to an ant sandwich. They began tickling and nipping him so Cheeko began to run quickly through the forest, brushing himself down as he ran, to get the rest of the ants off him.

Running amongst the trees he suddenly heard a loud 'WHOOSH,' his legs went from underneath him and he was whisked off the ground and hurled into the air. It was a trap, he had been caught in a net and was dangling in mid air. The net had been hidden amongst leaves and moss and Cheeko was well and truly stuck.

Holding onto his necklace he shouted; "never fear Tanga-Tanga is here," but nothing happened and he could barely move as the net had him trapped. Cheeko was very frightened and curled up into a tight little ball. Every so often he held his necklace and whispered Tanga-Tanga's name, but nothing happened.

Cheeko wondered if the same human from the shack had set the trap, he didn't want to go back there again. Burying himself under the leaves he put moss in his ears, so he couldn't hear anything that might frighten him. Darkness began to draw in and Cheeko was left dangling in the net feeling very lonely.

During the night he began to hear a very faint croaking sound, even though he had moss in his ears, he could still hear it. It reminded him of the sound tree frogs used to make at home and seemed to be coming from near his ear.

Cheeko turned to look and there sat on his shoulder was a fluorescent green speck about the size of a thumbnail. It was the same speck he had seen throughout his journey and was so bright he could see it had red eyes, black spots down its back and quite a large smile.

"Hello," it said in a squeaky voice.

"Hello, who are you?" asked Cheeko.

"My name is Speckles. I have been with you throughout your journey, for I am your guardian angel and guide your natural monkey instincts with my magical sparkling crystals."

"I have seen your puff of sparkling crystals. I thought it was the light playing tricks on me," said Cheeko.

74

"Fear not little monkey friend for I will be with you at all times, even when you cannot see me," said Speckles.

Speckles stayed with Cheeko all night. Every so often Cheeko saw a thin pink tongue poke out from the fluorescent green speck. It was a very long tongue for such a tiny frog and would zip out and catch tiny mozzies that not even Cheeko could see. Speckles would then roll his tongue back in and give out a little croak.

Next morning Cheeko began talking to Speckles, but there was no reply. Cheeko rummaged through his fur, as Speckles was so small he could be hiding anywhere, but he had disappeared.

Cheeko then poked his head up from the pile of leaves and gasped in horror. The rainbow had completely disappeared, gone forever along with his dream. His heart sank; "I have lost my family forever," he cried and a little tear ran down his sweet cheek.

Cheeko sank down to the bottom of the net and hid amongst the leaves. He put more moss into his ears and closed his eyes, he was feeling very sorry for himself and did not want to see or hear anything.

By late afternoon the sun was very hot, Cheeko was getting hungry and thirsty and feeling fed up. Then suddenly out of nowhere something hard hit him on the head, which really hurt.

Cheeko had to remain very quiet, as he did not know who, or what was out there. With moss still in his ears he could hear nothing and was too scared to peep. Cheeko just lay there very still, hidden amongst the leaves.

After a few seconds he could feel himself being lowered slowly to the ground. Cheeko froze with fear, he couldn't bear the thought of being captured again, his legs began to tremble and his knees began to knock.

Cheeko hit the ground with a big bump and shrieked loudly; "AAAHH," he quickly put his hand to his mouth to quieten himself. Cheeko looked around for his guardian angel, but Speckles was nowhere to be seen.

Something began rummaging in the net trying to get at Cheeko. He kept trying to dodge whatever it was, but four arms, not two, grabbed hold of him and pulled him out; Cheeko's knees still knocking in fear.

Looking like a compost heap with moss in his ears and leaves stuck to his head, Cheeko began to wipe the soil out of his eyes and he looked up. He could just about make out two little figures standing side by side, but his eyes were taking a while to focus properly and he couldn't see. These two figures looked quite small and furry, but also seemed very familiar.

After a few minutes his eyesight eventually cleared and Cheeko couldn't believe what he was seeing. He rubbed his eyes again in case he still had soil in them, or was imagining things. No the two figures still looked the same, furry and small and were definitely not humans.

Cheeko's eyes were now fully focused and there to his amazement, stood in front of him, were his two brothers; Coco and Maddy. Cheeko collapsed on the floor in disbelief, his brothers ran over to him and brushed all the leaves and soil off him.

"CHEEKO IS THAT YOU?" they both shrieked.

"Yes it is me," said Cheeko sobbing.

Cheeko could not believe he had been reunited with his brothers. Now it all began to make sense, the rainbow had started to disappear because he was getting nearer to finding his pot of gold, his family.

Coco and Maddy picked Cheeko up slowly, as his legs were still trembling from shock, and they all hugged one another.

"I should have known when something hit me on the head that it was you two little rascals," said Cheeko.

They all sat down on a log to gather their thoughts together, for they were very pleased and excited. It had been the worst time of Cheeko's life and now hopefully it was all over. He had been so scared that he would never see his family again and there right in front of him were his two brothers, the terrible twins. He could play games with them again like he used to.

"What happened to you Cheeko? We have all been so worried about you, we thought we would never see you again," said Coco.

"Oh it is a very long story and it's been a very long journey, let us just call it Cheeko's island adventure. One day I will tell you all about it, but for now I am just happy to see you again. Please take me to the rest of our family."

"Okay let's go. Mama will be so shocked, she has quietly shed a tear for you everyday Cheeko, ever since we were separated and papa, well we lost something in him the day you went missing. He has never been the same since, but now all that will change, we are reunited again," said Maddy.

Cheeko's journey had brought him to the foot of one of the mountains. He followed his brothers as they started to climb a hidden pathway, only big enough for small animals. On their way to the top of the mountain they swung through the trees like old times, chattering and laughing as they did so.

Eventually they all reached the top of the mountain and were surrounded by thick trees and bushes. These were so thick you could not see what lay on the other side.

Maddy started to crawl through the bushes, closely followed by Cheeko and Coco. The bushes seemed to go on forever until Maddy eventually disappeared out the other side. Cheeko followed, stood up, brushed himself down and looked up. To his amazement he was stood on the mountain he had seen whilst flying with the pelican.

This particular mountain was very special, it was once a volcano and fresh rainwater had gathered in a large crater in the centre of it. This was the glistening Cheeko had seen from high in the sky. The mountain was surrounded by palm and coconut trees and was a magnificent sight.

Cheeko then looked across to a secluded part of the mountain and could see the rest of his family going about their daily business. His mother, Tulum, was preparing food. Anya, his sister, was lazing around, lying in the sunshine and his father, Miguel, was sat on a log with his back to everybody, just being head of the family.

Cheeko could even see the mongooses sniffing amongst the leaves on the floor and scurrying off to their hideouts carrying juicy red berries. Tiny turquoise humming birds danced around brightly coloured flowers, collecting their pollen. It was alive with creatures of the forest going about their business, but more importantly they were all free.

Coco gave out a loud chatter to attract everyone's attention, they all suddenly stopped and looked around. They looked and looked, they all did a double-take and looked again.

"CHEEKO?" shouted his mother, "Cheeko, no it can't be?"

Cheeko gave out his high-pitched chatter and then everyone knew it was him. They all ran over, even the mongooses, and piled on top of him. His mother pulled him out from the bottom of the pile and squoze him giving him a big kiss. Tears ran down everyone's sweet cheeks.

The first thing his mother said to him was; "have you eaten Cheeko?"

"No mama not for days."

Tulum was horrified, for nobody ever went without food. She led him over to where she was preparing their usual family feast and served him a huge meal of all his favourites; big juicy berries, large bananas, mango fruit, all washed down with sweet coconut milk. After he had finished Cheeko's belly was so full it was poking out, it was the most he had eaten in months.

"We must throw a party tomorrow. I want everyone to know my Cheeko is home, safe and sound," announced his mother.

While everyone buzzed around planning his home coming party Cheeko fell asleep, for he could now sleep soundly knowing he was safe. He hadn't had a proper nights sleep in a long time and was soon snoring away peacefully. Tulum went over and covered him up with a large leaf to keep him warm.

Everyone slept close to Cheeko that night, for no one could quite believe that he was safely home.

The whole family rose early the next day, preparing for Cheeko's party. Cheeko sat on a log just watching, trying to take it all in. Nobody had asked him any questions about where he had been, or what had happened to him. At that point his father came over to the log and sat next to him.

"Good to have you home son."

"It's great to be back," said Cheeko.

"Tell us in your own time about your adventure."

"One day I will. Just one thing papa, have you ever heard of a Bonobo monkey?" asked Cheeko.

"Never heard of one, they don't exist Cheeko, no such thing," said Miguel. With that his father got up and went over to join in with the party preparations.

Cheeko looked down at his shell and took hold of it and thought to himself, with a sprinkling of monkey magic they do exist, they really do. He sat and pondered for a while thinking of Tanga-Tanga and what a great monkey he was, but was startled by an almighty squawk. Cheeko looked up and there perched in a tree, as bold as brass, sat Loretta.

"You took your time," she said sharply to Cheeko.

"Loretta, am I glad to see you. I thought I'd lost you forever. What happened, how did you get here?" shouted Cheeko.

"I was guided by puffs of sparkling crystals and a small speck of fluorescent light, I have been here for days," she said.

"I wondered who that bird belonged to, it just appeared and has been hanging around, watching us everyday," said Miguel.

"Family, this is Loretta. She is a beautiful parrot and was my friend and companion on my journey. Loretta, welcome to the family," said Cheeko and she flew down to join them.

Evening came and the party got into full swing. Everyone was dancing around a fire, singing and enjoying themselves, even Loretta. All the creatures of the forest joined in, it was so lively and jolly. Coco and

Maddy had made musical instruments out of coconut shells and were playing those, much to everyone's delight and amusement.

At one point it all got a bit too much for Cheeko. It would take him a while to get used to the buzzing activity of the forest again, for he had been used to darkness and loneliness for a long time.

Sitting on a log near the pond he watched the beautiful sun setting. The sky was bright orange and looked magnificent and he pondered for a while on all that had happened to him.

Cheeko couldn't help but feel sad at the thought of leaving his soul mate Sandy behind, from now on she would be in his dreams. On hearing a little croak he turned and saw Speckles disappearing into a puff of sparkling crystals. This must be his monkey instincts telling him to one day follow his dream and find Sandy and to always remember 'dreams turn tears into rainbows!'

Thanks to Tanga-Tanga he had found his family at the end of the rainbow, his pot of gold. Cheeko then got up off the log and went to join everyone and enjoy his new found freedom. This is where he and all the other animals belonged, living freely amongst the rainforest in peace and harmony.

The future for Cheeko, his family and all the animals of the forest and ocean was very uncertain. Who knew what lay ahead of them? It was probably only a matter of time before their homes and habitat were threatened and destroyed. One day though, if this destruction and devastation continued, there would be nowhere safe for them to run!

The End, for now!

Become a Cheeko Buddy

Cheeko would like to become a representative on behalf of the animals and promote wildlife/animal welfare and conservation awareness. To enable him to do this a sprinkling of monkey magic has brought him to life and Cheeko has been made into a soft toy.

Cheeko also has his own Facebook page and you can follow him at cheekos.adventure or on Twitter #CheekoBuddy @CheekoChatter and his website cheekosadventure.com

Become a Cheeko Buddy and follow the Cheeko Chatter; it's where 'dreams turn tears into rainbows!'

83

How You Can Help Cheeko's Friends!

Protecting primates and habitats worldwide

Cheeko is an Ambassador for Wild Futures and from the sale of every Cheeko's Island Adventure a donation will be made to Wild Futures monkey charity.

Wild Futures is a registered charity founded upon five decades of experience as a leader in the field of primate welfare and conservation, environmental education and sustainable practice. They are committed to protecting primates and habitats worldwide.

Wild Futures runs The Monkey Sanctuary in Cornwall, UK - a safe haven for monkeys rescued from situations of abuse and neglect, which has an international reputation for quality of care and innovative management techniques - www.monkeysanctuary.org

They work closely with other organisations to lobby local and central government to try and bring about positive change for primates. They also support projects overseas with advice, funding and practical assistance and believe that education is vital in changing things for the better; educating visitors to their sanctuary and more than 3,000 students on their work each year. The charity receives no government funding, so financial support is vital to allow them to continue their vital work. (Logo and text courtesy of Wild Futures).

If you are 16 or under you too can help Cheeko's little monkey friends and become a Young Ambassador for Wild Futures. To find out more information visit www.wildfutures.org

Cheeko's Wildlife Quiz

1) Do Bonobo monkeys, like Tanga-Tanga, really exist?
Yes or No

2) What age can giant tortoises, like Dillbert, live up to?
   a) **At least 300 years or more**
   b) **At least 200 years or more**
   c) **At least 100 years or more**

3) Do Macaw parrots, like Loretta, have their first and fourth toes pointing backwards?
Yes or No

4) Scoot is a sea turtle, how many species of sea turtle are there?
   a) **10**
   b) **5**
   c) **7**

5) Where was Speckles, the smallest frog in the world, discovered?
   a) **Papua New Guinea**
   b) **China**
   c) **Australia**

6) Cheeko is from the Vervet monkey family. What colour are the faces of Vervet monkeys?
   a) **Green**
   b) **Black**
   c) **Brown**

7) Sandy was a lonely dog until she met Cheeko. How many dogs are estimated to be in the world?
   a) **Between 700 million to over one billion**
   b) **Between 50 million to over 80 million**
   c) **Between 5 million to over 7 million**

85

8) What country is known as the land of the flying fish?
   a) **Africa**
   b) **Mexico**
   c) **Barbados**

9) What does Tanga-Tanga's full name, Tangakwunua, mean in Native America?

   a) **Gold**
   b) **Rainbow**
   c) **Dreams**

Answers on pages 87 and 88

 **Quiz Answers and Facts**

Question 1
Answer: Yes, Bonobo monkeys do exist
Bonobos are an endangered great ape and can be found in the Congo Basin in Democratic Republic of the Congo, in Central Africa. They are threatened by habitat destruction and poaching. They typically live 40 years in captivity, unknown how long they live until in the wild. (Source: en.m.wikipedia.org.wiki/Bonobo).

Question 2
Answer: c) Giant tortoises can live up to at least 100 years or more
Giant tortoises can be found in the Seychelles and Galapagos Islands in Ecuador. They can weigh up to 300kg (660lb) and grow to be 1.3m (4ft 3in) long. They are amongst the world's longest living animals. (Source: en.m.wikipedia.org.wiki/Giant_tortoise).

Question 3
Answer: Yes, Macaw parrots do have their first and fourth toes pointing backwards
The majority of Macaws are now endangered in the wild. Their facial feather pattern is as unique as a fingerprint. The greatest threat to the Macaw population is rapid rate of deforestation and illegal trapping. Native to Central America, especially Mexico and South America. (Source: en.m.wikipedia.org.wiki/Macaw).

Question 4
Answer: c) There are 7 species of sea turtle
The seven species of turtle are Leatherback, Green sea turtle, Loggerhead, Kemps Ridley, Hawksbill, Flatback and Olive Ridley. The Leatherback is the only sea turtle that doesn't have a hard shell. Instead it has bony plates beneath its leathery skin. It is the largest sea turtle, measuring 6 to 9 feet (1.8m to 2.7m) in length and 3 to 5 feet (0.91 to 1.52m) in width. At maturity sea turtles can weigh 1,500 pounds (680kg). (Source: en.m.wikipedia.org.wiki/Sea_turtle).

Question 5
Answer: a) Papua New Guinea
The world's smallest frog was discovered in August 2009 and is 7.7mm (0.30in) in length and is capable of jumping 30 times its body length. They live in leaf litter on the floors of tropical forests and are tinier than a penny. Their real name is Paedophryne Amauensis.
(Source: en.m.wikipedia.org.wiki/Paedophryne_amauensis).

Question 6
Answer: b) Black
Vervet monkeys live in social groups between 10 to 70 monkeys. They have four confirmed predators, being leopards, eagles, pythons and baboons. Vervets are believed to have up to 30 different alarm calls. They eat mainly a vegetarian diet consisting of wild fruit, flowers, leaves, seeds and seed pods. They are also known to eat grasshoppers and termites.
(Source: en.m.wikipedia.org.wiki/Vervet_monkey).

Question 7
Answer: a) Between 700 million to over one billion
The dog was the first domesticated animal. The father of a litter is called a Sire and the mother a Dam. A dog's average sleep time is 10.1 hours per day. Chocolate, onion, garlic, grapes and raisins are all poisonous to dogs. The breed with the shortest lifespan is the Dogue de Bordeaux, living approximately 5.2 years. The breeds with the longest lifespan include Toy Poodles, Japanese Spitz, Border Terriers and Tibetan Spaniels, living approximately 14 to 15 years.
(Source: en.m.wikipedia.org.wiki/dog).

Question 8
Answer: c) Barbados
The flying fish can make powerful self propelled leaps out of the water and into the air. Their long wing like fins enable them to glide above the water's surface. They can travel at speeds of more than 70km/h (43mph) and a maximum of 6m (20ft) above the sea's surface.
(Source: en.m.wikipedia.org.wiki/Flying_fish).

Question 9
Answer: b) Rainbow

**LOOK OUT FOR
CHEEKO'S AFRICAN ADVENTURE!
AVAILABLE IN 2016**

Details available at cheekosadventure.com

Lightning Source UK Ltd.
Milton Keynes UK
UKOW06f2345191015

260968UK00012B/49/P